THE ANIMALS

S E L E C T E D   P O E M S

THE ANIMALS

S E L E C T E D   P O E M S

by MICHIO MADO

decorations by MITSUMASA ANNO

translated by THE EMPRESS MICHIKO OF JAPAN

MARGARET K. McELDERRY BOOKS
New York
Maxwell Macmillan Canada · Toronto
Maxwell Macmillan International · New York · Oxford · Singapore · Sydney

Margaret K. McElderry Books
Macmillan Publishing Company
866 Third Avenue, New York, NY 10022

Maxwell Macmillan Canada, Inc.
1200 Eglinton Avenue East, Suite 200
Don Mills, Ontario M3C 3N1

Macmillan Publishing Company is part of the
Maxwell Communication Group of Companies.

Printed and bound in Japan by Toppan Printing Company
The English text of this book is set in Usherwood Medium.
The Japanese text of this book is set in BM-A-OKL.
The decorations are cut paper.

First edition
1   3   5   7   9   10   8   6   4   2

Library of Congress Cataloging-in-Publication Data
Mado, Michio, date. The animals : selected poems / Michio Mado ;
illustrated by Mitsumasa Anno ; translated by The Empress Michiko of
Japan. — 1st ed.   p.   cm.
Summary: A collection of twenty poems about animals, including the
peacock, giraffe, and sea cucumber. Includes both Japanese and English
text.
ISBN 0-689-50574-4
1. Mado, Michio, date.—Translations into English.   2. Animals—
Juvenile poetry.   [1. Animals—Poetry.   2. Japanese
poetry.   3. Japanese language materials—Bilingual.]   I. Anno,
Mitsumasa, date, ill.   II. Michiko, Empress, consort of Akihito,
Emperor of Japan, date.   III. Title.
PL833.A26A25   1992   895.6'15—dc20   92-10356

"Little Elephant" and "Waves and Shells" have been used by
permission of JASRAC License 91660-34-101.

もくじ　CONTENTS

ことり

そらの
しずく？

うたの
つぼみ？

目でなら
さわっても　いい？

A LITTLE BIRD

A dewdrop
from the sky?

A bud
of a song?

May I touch you
Just with my eye?

スワン

みえています

なにかの　しあわせで
とくべつに
みえているかのように

A SWAN

You stand out clearly

As if some sort of joy
Made you
Especially visible

クジャク

ひろげた　はねの
まんなかで
クジャクが　ふんすいに
なりました
さらさらさらと
まわりに　まいて　すてた
ほうせきを　見てください
いま
やさしい　こころの　ほかには
なんにも　もたないで
うつくしく
やせて　立っています

A PEACOCK

★

At the center
Of his widely spread feathers
The peacock has become a fountain.
Look at all those jewels
He's jetted and given away,
Strewing them all around.

Now with nothing left for himself
But his loving heart,
The peacock stands
Beautiful
And slim.

ヒバリ

あの　青い
空の　かがみの

どこかに　あたしが
うつって　いるかしら

あ　あんな　遠くに
こめつぶのように

ここで　しずかな
あたしの　うたが

あそこからは
にぎやかそうに　ひびくこと

A SKYLARK

Somewhere
In that blue sky

Am I reflected
As in a mirror,

There, so far away,
Me like a tiny, tiny grain?

Then, from up there,
Resound your trilling notes,

An echo to the song
I sing here all alone.

いい　けしき

水が　よこたわっている
水平に

木が　立っている
垂直に

山が　坐っている
じつに水平に
じつに垂直に

この平安をふるさとにしているのだ
ぼくたち
ありとあらゆる生き物が…

A PLEASANT LANDSCAPE

★

Water lies
Horizontally

The tree stands
Perpendicularly

The mountain sits up
Very horizontally
Very perpendicularly

This peaceful stability
Is home to us,
To us creatures of all sorts

ああ　どこかから

庭を　とおって
ゆうびんやさんが　かえっていく

きょうも　みおくっているのは
屋根の　スズメと
かきねの　デンデンムシだ

「ごめんよ
　きみたちあての　手がみは
　来てないんだ」
というように
ゆうびんやさんは
そそくさ　いっちゃった

ああ　どこかから
こないかなあ

なの花びらのような　手がみと
マメのような　こづつみが
——ゆうびんって

スズメたちに
デンデンムシたちに

AH, FROM SOMEWHERE . . .

Through the garden
The mailman is on his way out.

It is always
The sparrows on the roof
And the snails in the hedge
Who see him off.

But, as if telling them,
    "Sorry, no letters for you,"
The mailman hurries away.

Ah, could it not happen
That from somewhere
Will come a letter and a package
For those sparrows and snails,
With the mailman calling,
    "Here you are!"

A letter
Like a flower petal,
A package
Like a bean?

ぞうさん

ぞうさん
ぞうさん
おはなが　ながいのね
　そうよ
　かあさんも　ながいのよ

ぞうさん
ぞうさん
だあれが　すきなの
　あのね
　かあさんが　すきなのよ

LITTLE ELEPHANT

"Little elephant,
 Little elephant,
 What a long nose you have."
   "Sure it's long.
     So is my mommy's."

"Little elephant,
 Little elephant,
 Tell me who you like."
   "I like mommy,
     I like her the most."

シマウマ

手製の
おりに
はいっている

ZEBRA

In a cage
Of his
Own making

キリン

みおろす　キリンと
みあげる　ぼくと
あくしゅ　したんだ
めと　めで　ぴかっと…

そしたら
せかいじゅうが
しーんと　しちゃってさ
こっちを　みたよ

GIRAFFE

The giraffe looked down,
I looked up.
Flash!
Our eyes met,
Something clicked between us.

Hushed in wonder,
Everyone was looking at us.

トンボ

トンボを　つかまえたのと
「いたいっ！」
と　逃がしてしまったのと同時だった

指先に　かみついた歯の光が
一しゅん
目を　射た

が　それはトンボのではなく
あんなに今　けろっとしている
あの青空の　歯だったようでならない

DRAGONFLY

No sooner had I caught the dragonfly
Than I let it go
With a loud, "Ouch!"

Like a flash, the shining teeth
That bit me on my fingertip
Hit my eyes.

Was it really the teeth of the dragonfly?
Was it not the bright light of that blue sky
Now looking so totally indifferent?

チョウチョウ

こころなら
こんなに　きれいなの…

そう　いって
でてくるのかしら
もじゃもじゃけむしから
いつも
チョウチョウは

A BUTTERFLY

"My heart, you see, is lovely,"
You seem
To be saying
When you emerge transformed
From a hairy caterpillar's cocoon.

Am I right,
Butterfly?

チョウチョウ

チョウチョウは
ねむる　とき
はねを　たたんで　ねむります

だれの　じゃまにも　ならない
あんなに　小さな　虫なのに
それが　また　はんぶんに　なって
そっと…

だれだって　それを見ますと
せかいじゅうに
しーっ！
と　めくばせ　したくなります

どんなに　かすかな　もの音でも
チョウチョウの　ねむりを
やぶりはしないかと…

BUTTERFLIES

★

Butterflies close their wings
When they go to sleep.
They are so small,
In nobody's way,
Yet they fold themselves
In half
Modestly…

Watching them behave in such a manner,
One cannot help
But nod at the whole world,
And say, "Hush!"

Anxious
Lest even the slightest sound
Should disturb the sleep of the butterflies.

イヌが歩く

イヌが歩く
四つの足で

どの足のつぎに
どの足が動くのか
どんなに見ていても　わからない

音のちがうすずを
どの足にも
一つずつ

ちりん
ころん
からん
ぽろん

むすんでやったら
わかるかな

A DOG WALKS

A dog walks
On four legs.

I can never tell,
Though I watch closely,
Which leg
Comes after which.

How about tying
On each leg a bell,
Each with a different sound?

ChiRin
KoRon
KaRan
PoRon

Then shall I know?

なみと　かいがら

うずまきかいがら
どうして　できた
──なみが　ぐるぐる
　　うずまいて　できた

ももいろかいがら
どうして　できた
──なみが　きんきら
　　ゆうやけて　できた

まんまるかいがら
どうして　できた
──なみが　まんまるい
　　あわ　たてて　できた

WAVES AND SHELLS

Spiral shell, how were you born?
    I was born
While the waves were whirling
Round and round.

Pink shell, how were you born?
    I was born
While the waves were shining
Under the sunset glow.

Round shell, how were you born?
    I was born
While the waves were bubbling
Foamy froth.

ねむり

わたしの　からだの
ちいさな　ふたつの　まどに
しずかに
ブラインドが　おりる　よる

せかいじゅうの
そらと　うみと　りくの
ありとあらゆる　いのちの
ちいさな　ふたつずつの　まどに
しずかに
ブラインドが　おりる

どんなに　ちいさな
ひとつの　ゆめも
ほかの　ゆめと
ごちゃごちゃに　ならないように

SLEEP

At night,
When quietly
The two tiny windows of my body
Lower their blinds,

The two tiny windows
Of all creatures of all kinds,
Living in the sky,
The sea, and on land,
Quietly
Lower their blinds, too,

So as not to cause
A single dream

To be mixed
With any other.

イナゴ

はっぱにとまった
イナゴの目に
一てん
もえている夕やけ

でも　イナゴは
ぼくしか見ていないのだ
エンジンをかけたまま
いつでもにげられるしせいで……

ああ　強い生きものと
よわい生きもののあいだを
川のように流れる
イネのにおい！

A LOCUST

The eye of a locust
Perched on a green blade
Reflects
The fiery glow of the setting sun.

But what the eye really sees
Is me,
For the locust's ready to take flight,
With its engine on.

Ah, the smell of the rice paddy
Flows like a river between us,
Between us,
The strong and the weak.

ナマコ

ナマコは　だまっている
でも
「ぼく　ナマコだよ」って
いってるみたい

ナマコの　かたちで
いっしょうけんめいに…

A SEA CUCUMBER

A sea cucumber says nothing,
Yet it seems to be saying,
"I'm a sea cucumber,"
With all its vigor and energy

By simply being
A sea cucumber

アリ

アリを見ると
アリに　たいして
なんとなく
もうしわけ　ありません
みたいなことに　なる

いのちの　大きさは
だれだって
おんなじなのに
こっちは　そのいれものだけが
こんなに
ばかでかくって……

AN ANT

Watching an ant
I often feel
Like voicing an apology
Toward this little being.

Life is life to any creature
Big or small.
The difference is only
In the size of its container,
And mine happens to be so ridiculously,
Enormously big.

ヤマバト

耳を　すますと
もう　きこえない

わすれていると
ほら　また　よぶ

雨に　けむる
山のほうで

あんなに　ことしも
春が　夏を

あんなに　がんこに
大昔の　なまりで

それで　なければ
つうじないかのように

ほーぽー　ぐるる
ほーぽー　ぐるる

A TURTLE DOVE

Once I try to listen
It's no longer heard.

Once I stop heeding
It starts again to call—

Somewhere near the mountain
Misty in the rain—

The annual, unchanging call
Of spring to summer

Stubbornly the same
From ancient days

As if in no other way
Can the call communicate.

Hō Pō, GruRu
Ho Pō, GruRu

どうぶつたち

いつのころから
こういうことに　なったのか
きがついて　みると
みんなが
あちらのほうを　むいている
ひとの　いないほうを

にじのように　はなれて……

THE ANIMALS

★

How and since when
Has it been like this?
When we begin to see,
They've turned their backs to us,
Facing away from where we are.

They are now so far away,
As apart from us as is the rainbow.

AFTERWORD

UNTIL VERY RECENTLY the rich tradition of Japanese children's literature, including poetry for children, has remained virtually unknown outside of Japan. It is like a treasure waiting to be discovered.

It was a decision by the Japanese Section of the International Board on Books for Young People (JBBY) to nominate the poetry of Michio Mado for the 1990 Hans Christian Andersen Award that began the search for a translator of his works. Even the most popular of Michio Mado's poems were not available in any other language.

JBBY sought the help of Her Majesty Empress Michiko because, as a composer of *waka*, the traditional Japanese poem of five-seven-five-seven-seven syllables, she is a poet in her own right, and because Her Majesty has been translating Japanese poems into English with great sensitivity since 1975.

To our joy, Her Majesty gave us a helping hand, and despite her heavy schedule of official duties, she managed to find time, here and there, to select, translate, and arrange these poems taken from Mado's three volumes to produce a simple, hand-bound book titled *Animals* that was the manuscript of this book.

Mitsumasa Anno has decorated this pioneering volume with elaborate and beautiful cut-paper work.

We are grateful for the talent and cooperation of these special people. They have made our dream of sharing Japanese children's poetry with the children of the world come true.

TAYO SHIMA
JBBY Board Member
Director, Musée Imaginaire